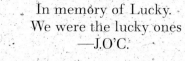

In memory of Lucky.
We were the lucky ones
—J.O'C.

To my favorite boy, Sam, and
our favorite poodle, Clementine
—J.H.

VIKING
Published by the Penguin Group
Penguin Putnam Books for Young Readers,
345 Hudson Street, New York, New York 10014,
U.S.A.

Penguin Books Ltd, Registered Offices:
Harmondsworth, Middlesex, England

First published in 2005 by Viking,
a division of Penguin Putnam
Books for Young Readers.

1 3 5 7 9 10 8 6 4 2

LIBRARY OF CONGRESS
CATALOGING-IN-PUBLICATION DATA
O'Connor, Jane.
The perfect puppy for me /
by Jane O'Connor and Jessie Hartland ;
illustrated by Jessie Hartland.
p.   cm.
Summary: While waiting to get his very own
puppy, a young boy spends time with various dogs
and describes what the different breeds are like.
ISBN 0-670-03614-5
[1. Dogs—Fiction. 2. Pets—Fiction.]
I. Hartland, Jessie, ill. II. Title.
PZ7.O222 Pe 2003
[E]—dc21
2002015568

Manufactured in China
Set in Walbaum

Thanks to Danielle Dalton, D.V.M.,
for vetting the manuscript.

VIKING

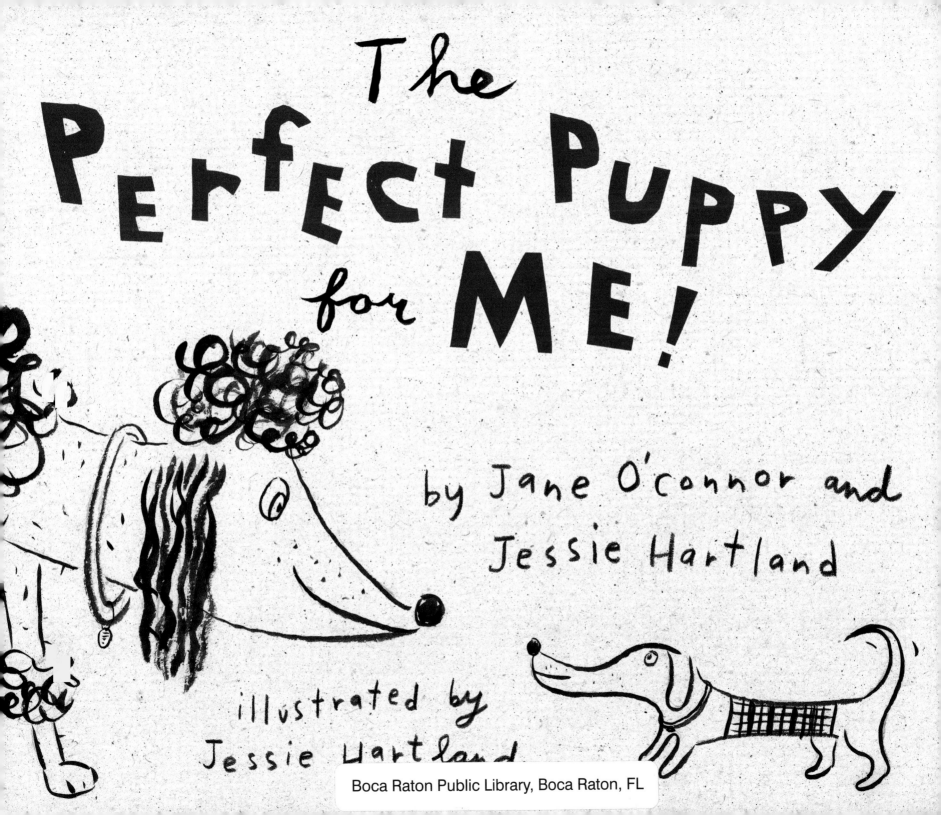

The PERFECT PUPPY for ME!

by Jane O'connor and
Jessie Hartland

illustrated by
Jessie Hartland

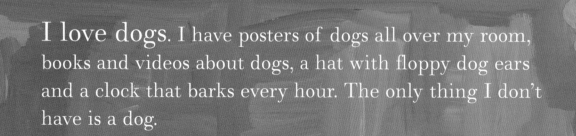

I love dogs. I have posters of dogs all over my room, books and videos about dogs, a hat with floppy dog ears and a clock that barks every hour. The only thing I don't have is a dog.

But for my next birthday I am going to get one. By then I will know what kind of dog is perfect for me and my family.

Guess what is missing?

Dad   me   my sister   mom

Duke
the German shepherd

Vera, who lives next door, has a big German shepherd named Duke. Vera calls him "Kind Sir," because he carries in her groceries from the car.

German shepherds are very friendly. They are also brave, loyal, and smart—that's why they make good police dogs and guide dogs for blind people. But they need a lot of space to run around. I don't think our yard is big enough.

Dogs and wolves belong to the same animal family— CANIDS.

POKER
the Basset Hound

Poker's nicknames are:

"Pokey,"

"slow poke",

and

"couch potato."

Poker's favorite foods are potato chips and Fig Newtons

Don't feed a dog from the table. They become terrible beggars if you do.

My best friend Joey has a six-year-old basset hound named Poker. Poker is sweet but lazy. Joey has to drag Poker outside for a walk.

Here is what POKER likes to do:

sleep   nap   snooze   rest

Besides sleeping, Poker loves to eat. He always knows when Joey is putting food in his dish. I read that dogs can smell about a million times better than people can. The vet said that Poker has to lose seven pounds. So Poker gets diet dog food. Every week there's a weigh-in.

Here's how you weigh a DOG:

Together we weigh 138 lbs.

Alone I weigh 85 lbs.

$$\begin{array}{r} 138 \\ -85 \\ \hline 53 \end{array}$$

Poker weighs 53 lbs.

All tired out after weigh-in

DANISH the Great Dane

Our science teacher's dog had puppies. Great Danes are huge, but the puppies were tiny. Nobody could get too near them. Danish might think that we were going to hurt them and snap at us.

Mother dogs are very loving and protective.

DANISH

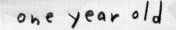
one year old

Newborn

They can't see,
hear,
walk,
or even wag their tails.

six weeks old

They can run
and jump
and play
and make high
little baby barks.

ten weeks old

Ready to go to
a new home.

full grown.

A female dog is pregnant for two months before she has her litter—that means all the puppies born at one time. Danish was feeding the puppies her milk. Soon their baby teeth will start coming in. Puppies lose their baby teeth, just like kids do.

Maybe there is a dog tooth fairy.

PATSY
the
Newfoundland

Newfies' webbed feet help them swim.

This summer when we rented a cabin, the family next door had a Newfoundland and a Jack Russell terrier. Patsy was great. But we don't have a pool, and, like all Newfies, Patsy loved to swim.

Patsy shaking herself dry.

Newfies like shade.

They drool a lot.

Their greasy coats are waterproof.

I think Newfies

look kind of like BEARS.

Do you know that dogs are born knowing how to "doggy paddle"?
Patsy always made sure I wasn't in over my head. Newfies are like that.
There are many true stories about Newfies rescuing drowning people.

TIDBIT
the
JACK RUSSELL
Terrier

Jack Russells are named after an Englishman who lived in the 1800s. He bred these spunky little dogs to go fox hunting.

Tidbit had a ton of energy. She would race around in circles, stop, then leap way up in the air. What a nutball! Tidbit loved chasing animals. Once she caught a bird. Gross! Tidbit acted like a big dog trapped in the body of a small dog.

One time Tidbit chased a skunk and got sprayed. She had to have a tomato juice bath... It's the only thing that gets out the stink.

She was always bossing Patsy around. She'd poke Patsy to make her wake up and play. When dogs are around each other, they always know who is the alpha or top dog. Tidbit was definitely top dog.

JACKPOT
the
Yellow Labrador

I have a dog-sitting job. Jackpot was lonely while his owner was at work. Dogs are social animals and need to be part of a "pack"—a group of other dogs or people. Labradors are retrievers: Jackpot can play fetch forever. Labs are also good around little kids. Once my sister stepped on Jackpot's paw; he didn't even growl.

Labs shed like crazy.

I don't mind.

Dogs don't sweat.

They pant with their tongues hanging out.

ALL dogs sleep

about 16 hours a day.

An hour after I feed Jackpot, I take him to the dog run. I bring a plastic bag along for poop. On the way, we often meet a lady named Harriet and her standard poodle, Claudine. First Jackpot and Claudine smell each other's noses. Then they smell each other's butts. That's how dogs say hello.

Tail position is a good sign of a dog's feelings:

TAIL

fearful

friendly, happy

tense, threatened

slow wag

tentative

Claudine the Poodle

where's the Kitty?

?

cats are not social animals.
They like to be off by themselves.

Claudine!
Bath time!

Poodles are smart. You can teach them to play hide-and-seek.
Poodles don't shed. They make good pets for people who are
allergic to dog fur. Claudine goes to a special dog beauty parlor
for a trim. She also has to be brushed and combed every day.

all dogs should
get bathed
about once
a month

Claudine

poodles
come
in
3
sizes:

standard

miniature

toy

One time, Harriet was baking cookies and left two sticks of butter out. Five minutes later—gone! We knew it was Claudine. All dogs are meat-eaters. But Claudine likes butter and cheese more than anything.

Never feed chocolate to a dog. They can't digest it.

It's like poison to them. macadamia nuts and onions are bad, too.

Harriet's Delicious Cookies for Dogs

(Have a grownup help you with the oven.)

2 cups flour   2 Tbs. melted butter
1 cup grated cheese   3/4 cup milk

Mix all the ingredients together. Knead the dough. Divide it in two parts and roll out to one inch thick. Cut into bone shapes. Place cookies on a cookie sheet and bake them at 375° for 12-15 minutes. Cool and serve. Makes a dozen.

yum
yum
yum

Goulash the mongrel

Goulash is a mongrel—a mix of many different kinds of dogs. Mrs. Fisher adopted her from an animal shelter right after Christmas. People sometimes get a dog as a Christmas present and then decide that it's too much work and leave it at a shelter. I am glad that Goulash got such a good home.

Goulash is: easygoing ... gentle ... sneaky... and always looking for love

Mrs. Fisher is trying to teach Goulash to behave better.

Dolly the Dachshund

My uncle Willy lives in New York City with his dachshund, Dolly. Every April and October there's a dachshund parade in Washington Square Park, and we take Dolly in her little hot dog bun cart. Can you find her?

HOT DOGS

I ♥ NY

Venezia

Dachshunds are good city dogs. They don't need much exercise, and they are happy in small apartments, but if Dolly wasn't in her bun, could she keep up with me?

Dollface
the
BULLdog

Before Dolly, Uncle Willy had a bulldog named Dollface. She died two years ago. I still miss her. When we'd take Dollface for a walk, everybody would stop, look, and laugh. Bulldogs are so funny looking that they are adorable. They are also smart and very patient with small children.

Her nicknames were "Dragon Breath" and "Gorgeous"*

Heat is very bad for bulldogs.

* you have to say it like this "gaw-juss."

pee yew

They are also gassy.

They are slow moving and don't like to be outside a long time. Bulldogs get sick a lot. They often have breathing problems. Dollface was only nine when she died. Other breeds can live much longer. I want a dog who will live a long, long, long time.

WINSTON

the
Cavalier
King Charles
Spaniel

Winston belongs to my uncle's neighbor. Winston has a pedigree: his parents and grandparents and great-grandparents were all the same breed he is and there are papers to prove it. Some dogs were bred to do a special job, like rounding up sheep. But Cavaliers are a toy breed. That means they were bred just to be pets.

combing and applying hairspray

SIR Winston

brushing

nail-clipping

Last February we went to the Westminster Dog Show in New York City. Winston was in the show. He's a very nice dog, but I don't care whether the dog we get has a pedigree.

Winston didn't win a prize this time.

Best IN Show

the winner!

Great news! Great news! Great news!

I am getting a puppy. Claudine
had a litter of puppies. And
guess who the father is? Jackpot!
The puppies are

Labradoodles

That means they are half Labrador and half
Standard poodle. I wanted to take all of them
home, but after we watched the puppies, we
decided on one that seemed the friendliest, and
was very calm.

This puppy is
the one we
picked.

claudine

JACKPOT

We got a lead, a collar, lots of puppy food, and a crate with a soft pillow.

Now all our puppy needs is a name.

Belka

Strelka

CLEM

DOGS

DOGS

all about the DOG

Doodle

DOODLE

She's got a name! Doodle. That's how my little sister said Labradoodle, and it stuck. Now Doodle has a new pack— us! I love her already. I know there's no such thing as a perfect dog . . . but Doodle is definitely the perfect puppy for me.

← Doodle's favorite toy